KT-225-161

ROBERT LOUIS STEVENSON

A Child's Garden of Verses

Decorations by

EVE GARNETT

PUFFIN BOOKS

PUFFIN BOOKS

Published by the Penguin Group
Penguin Books Ltd, 27 Wrights Lane, London W8 5TZ, England
Penguin Books USA Inc., 375 Hudson Street, New York, New York 10014, USA
Penguin Books Australia Ltd, Ringwood, Victoria, Australia
Penguin Books Canada Ltd, 10 Alcorn Avenue, Toronto, Ontario, Canada M4V 3B2
Penguin Books (NZ) Ltd, 182–190 Wairau Road, Auckland 10, Middlesex, England

Penguin Books Ltd, Registered Offices: Harmondsworth, Middlesex, England

First published 1885
Published in Puffin Books 1948
New edition 1952
Reissued 1994
3 5 7 9 10 8 6 4 2

All rights reserved

Filmset by Datix International Limited, Bungay, Suffolk
Printed in England by Clays Ltd, St Ives plc
Set in 12/15 pt Monophoto Plantin

Except in the United States of America, this book is sold subject
to the condition that it shall not, by way of trade or otherwise, be lent,
re-sold, hired out, or otherwise circulated without the publisher's
prior consent in any form of binding or cover other than that in
which it is published and without a similar condition including this
condition being imposed on the subsequent purchaser

A CHILD'S GARDEN OF VERSES

ROBERT LOUIS STEVENSON (1850–94) was born into a famous Edinburgh engineering family. His middle name was originally Lewis, but Robert changed the spelling, while keeping the pronunciation. His father wanted him to become an engineer, but Robert's constant ill health pushed him towards an indoor job. After studying law, he was called to the Scottish Bar in 1875; but he made little effort as a lawyer, since he was already trying to make his mark in the world of literature. He published a number of essays and articles and accounts of travels: he travelled widely all his life, in search of a climate which suited him. Success eluded him, however, until 1883 when *Treasure Island* was published.

Where all the greatest writers for children are concerned, it is probably true to say that the child-in-them never died. Nothing illustrates this better in the case of Robert Louis Stevenson than *A Child's Garden of Verses*. Published when he was thirty-five years old, every poem without exception captures the freshness, innocence and beauty of a child's vision of the world. It is clear that the 'child' in the title refers as much to the author as to any of the thousands of children who have enjoyed reading the poems over the years.

Stevenson was vivacious with a strong voice and gestures, but he was abnormally thin. He was in fact more or less an invalid from the 1880s onward and probably suffered from tuberculosis. In the late 1880s he left California for a holiday with his family in the Polynesian islands of the Pacific, fell in love with the islands, settled on Samoa and never left. The natives called him Tusitala, which means 'teller of tales'. He is buried high on a Samoan hill and his grave bears the following moving epitaph:

> Here he lies where he longed to be;
> Home is the sailor, home from the sea,
> And the hunter home from the hill.

Some other Puffin Classics to enjoy

PETER PAN
J M Barrie

SELECTED CAUTIONARY VERSES
Hilaire Belloc

ALICE'S ADVENTURES IN WONDERLAND
THROUGH THE LOOKING GLASS
Lewis Carroll

PINOCCHIO
Carlo Collodi

Contents

How the Verses were Written   ix

Dedication   xiii

Bed in Summer   1

A Thought   2

At the Seaside   3

Young Night Thought   4

Whole Duty of Children   5

Rain   6

Pirate Story   7

Foreign Lands   8

Windy Nights   10

Travel   11

Singing   14

Looking Forward   15

A Good Play   15

Where Go the Boats?   16

Auntie's Skirts   17

The Land of Counterpane   17

The Land of Nod   18

My Shadow   19

System   21

A Good Boy   22

Escape at Bedtime   23

Marching Song   24

The Cow   25

Happy Thought   26

The Wind   27

Keepsake Mill   28

Good and Bad Children   30

Foreign Children   33

The Sun's Travels   34

The Lamplighter   35

My Bed is a Boat   37

The Moon   38

The Swing   39

Time to Rise   40

Looking-glass River   41

Fairy Bread   43

From a Railway Carriage   44

Winter-time   45

The Hayloft   47

Farewell to the Farm   48

North-west Passage:

    1   Good Night   50

    2   Shadow March   50

    3   In Port   52

THE CHILD ALONE

The Unseen Playmate   57

My Ship and I   59

My Kingdom   60

Picture-books in Winter   62

My Treasures   64

Block City   65

The Land of Story-books   67

Armies in the Fire   69

The Little Land   70

GARDEN DAYS

Night and Day   77
Nest Eggs   80
The Flowers   83
Summer Sun   84
The Dumb Soldier   85
Autumn Fires   87
The Gardener   88
Historical Associations   89

ENVOYS

To Willie and Henrietta   95
To My Mother   96
To Auntie   97
To Minnie   98
To My Name-child   102
To Any Reader   104

Index of First Lines   107

How the Verses were Written

'These are rhymes, jingles; I don't go in for eternity and the three unities.' Robert Louis Stevenson wrote to his friend Sydney Colvin of these verses, 'I would just as soon call 'em "*Rimes for Children*" as anything else. I am not proud nor particular.'

And he told his devoted old nurse, Alison Cunningham – 'Cummy' as he called her – that the little book was all about his childhood and should, therefore, be dedicated to no other person 'but you who did so much to make that childhood happy . . . and as the only person who will really understand it.' . . . 'Of course,' he went on, 'this is only a flourish, like taking off one's hat, but still a person who has taken the trouble to write things, does not dedicate them to anyone without meaning it; and you must try to take this dedication in place of a great many things I might have said and ought to have done.'

Cummy had stayed with him throughout his childhood, which he described as being 'in reality a very mixed experience, full of fever, nightmare, insomnia, painful days, and interminable nights; and I can speak with less authority of gardens than of that other land of counterpane.'

Always delicate, he was subject as a child to attacks of croup – that dreaded haunter of Victorian homes – and other bronchial troubles; but he was fortunate in his nurse, who watched over him through the interminable nights, diverting him and indulging herself – for she had a great love of and feeling for words – by repeating in her rich Lowland accent, hymns, the metrical versions of the Psalms and the old tales of the Covenanters. One of young Louis's favourite games was to play at being Minister and holding Service in the Kirk.

The first batch of these verses came to him at Braemar in the intervals of writing *The Sea Cook, or Treasure Island, a Story for Boys,* as he called it while it was still in its early chapters. The words were running off his pen as fast as his hand could shape the letters. It was a glorious moment of creation and achievement. He was confident of success and had his young stepson, Lloyd Osbourne, beside him, providing an enthusiastic audience.

During the next four years (from 1881 to 1884) the rest of the rhymes were written, some in sadly different circumstances; as when he lay in the half darkness of a sickroom at Hyères with his right arm tied to his side to lessen the risk of further haemorrhage. He was accustomed to illness; and as he lay there, unable to read, hardly able to speak, his mind must surely have wandered back into those vivid memories of far-off days to pass the time, recalling with the peculiar clearness that comes in illness, not only the great occasions but also the little things, the smell of frost, the look of his own small footprints in new snow, the feel of darkness, the brilliance of spring days and the richness of summer.

Was it from a memory of himself sailing boats on the Water of Leith, that he wrote 'Where Go the Boats?', playing, as he often must have done, while staying with his grandfather at the Manse at Colinton?

'Do you remember,' he asked Cummy, 'making the whistle at Mount Chessie? I do not think it *was* my knife; I believe it was yours; but rhyme is a great monarch and goes before honesty, in these affairs at least.' This little incident is told in 'My Treasures' (see page 64).

Those years at the end of the seventies and the beginning of the eighties were rich ones for children with their annual yield of lovely picture-books by Randolph Caldecott, Kate Greenaway, and Walter Crane, cheap to buy but beautifully produced. New ideas were in the air, and it was suggested that Stevenson should provide a volume of stories for Caldecott to illustrate. He was thrilled with the idea, but somehow it came to nothing and, when his Verses were ready to be illustrated, Caldecott's health was already giving way (he died in the February of 1884) and Stevenson suggested either of the other great names, preferably Crane, as artist; but this, too, came to nothing, and the book was published in the spring of 1885 without any pictures.

Much had happened since those joyful days when the first verses were written and Stevenson hardly knew whether to be pleased or otherwise when he first looked on the completed volume; but he had caught the spirit of those childish experiences so truly that he could not be cast down for long and though he wrote to Edmund Gosse: 'I have now published, on 101 small pages, *The Complete Proof of Mr R. L. Stevenson's Incapacity to Write Verses* . . . They look ghastly in the cold light of print!' yet he had also to admit that there was 'something nice in the little ragged regiment' and that 'they seem to me to smile, to have a kind of childish treble note that sounds in my ears freshly – not song, if you will, but a child's voice.'

ELEANOR GRAHAM

Note: The quotations are all taken from *The Letters of Robert Louis Stevenson*, edited by Sydney Colvin.

Dedication
TO ALISON CUNNINGHAM
FROM HER BOY

For the long nights you lay awake
And watched for my unworthy sake:
For your most comfortable hand
That led me through the uneven land:
For all the story-books you read,
For all the pains you comforted,
For all you pitied, all you bore,
In sad and happy days of yore:–
My second Mother, my first Wife,
The angel of my infant life –
From the sick child, now well and old,
Take, nurse, the little book you hold!

And grant it, Heaven, that all who read
May find as dear a nurse at need,
And every child who lists my rhyme,
In the bright fireside, nursery clime,
May hear it in as kind a voice
As made my childish days rejoice!
R. L. S.

BED IN SUMMER

In winter I get up at night
And dress by yellow candle-light.
In summer, quite the other way,
I have to go to bed by day.

I have to go to bed and see
The birds still hopping on the tree,
Or hear the grown-up people's feet
Still going past me in the street.

And does it not seem hard to you,
When all the sky is clear and blue,
And I should like so much to play,
To have to go to bed by day?

A THOUGHT

It is very nice to think
The world is full of meat and drink,
With little children saying grace
In every Christian kind of place.

AT THE SEASIDE

When I was down beside the sea
A wooden spade they gave to me
   To dig the sandy shore.
My holes were empty like a cup,
In every hole the sea came up
   Till it could come no more.

YOUNG NIGHT THOUGHT

All night long, and every night,
When my mamma puts out the light,
I see the people marching by,
As plain as day, before my eye.

Armies and emperors and kings,
All carrying different kinds of things,
And marching in so grand a way,
You never saw the like by day.

So fine a show was never seen
At the great circus on the green;
For every kind of beast and man
Is marching in that caravan.

At first they move a little slow,
But still the faster on they go,
And still beside them close I keep
Until we reach the town of Sleep.

WHOLE DUTY OF CHILDREN

A child should always say what's true,
And speak when he is spoken to,
And behave mannerly at table:
At least as far as he is able.

Rain

The rain is raining all around,
It falls on field and tree,

It rains on the umbrellas here,
And on the ships at sea.

PIRATE STORY

Three of us afloat in the meadow by the swing,
   Three of us aboard in the basket on the lea.
Winds are in the air, they are blowing in the
      spring,
   And waves are on the meadows like the waves
      there are at sea.

Where shall we adventure, to-day that we're
      afloat,
   Wary of the weather and steering by a star?
Shall it be to Africa, a-steering of the boat,
   To Providence, or Babylon, or off to Malabar?

Hi! but here's a squadron a-rowing on the sea –
   Cattle on the meadow a-charging with a roar!
Quick, and we'll escape them, they're as mad as
      they can be.
   The wicket is the harbour and the garden is the
      shore.

Foreign Lands

Up into the cherry-tree
Who should climb but little me?
I held the trunk with both my hands
And looked abroad on foreign lands.

I saw the next-door garden lie,
Adorned with flowers before my eye,
And many pleasant places more
That I had never seen before.

I saw the dimpling river pass
And be the sky's blue looking-glass;
The dusty roads go up and down
With people tramping in to town.

If I could find a higher tree
Farther and farther I should see,
To where the grown-up river slips
Into the sea among the ships,

To where the roads on either hand
Lean onward into fairy land,
Where all the children dine at five,
And all the playthings come alive.

WINDY NIGHTS

Whenever the moon and stars are set,
　　Whenever the wind is high,
All night long in the dark and wet,
　　A man goes riding by.
Late in the night when the fires are out,
Why does he gallop and gallop about?

Whenever the trees are crying aloud,
　　And ships are tossed at sea,
By, on the highway, low and loud,
　　By at the gallop goes he.
By at the gallop he goes, and then
By he comes back at the gallop again.

TRAVEL

I should like to rise and go
Where the golden apples grow;
Where below another sky
Parrot islands anchored lie,
And, watched by cockatoos and goats,
Lonely Crusoes building boats;
Where in sunshine reaching out
Eastern cities, miles about,
Are with mosque and minaret
Among sandy gardens set,
And the rich goods from near and far
Hang for sale in the bazaar;
Where the Great Wall round China goes,
And on one side the desert blows,
And with bell and voice and drum,
Cities on the other hum;

Where are forests, hot as fire,
Wide as England, tall as a spire,
Full of apes and coco-nuts
And the negro hunters' huts;
Where the knotty crocodile
Lies and blinks in the Nile,
And the red flamingo flies
Hunting fish before his eyes;
Where in jungles, near and far,
Man-devouring tigers are,
Lying close and giving ear
Lest the hunt be drawing near,
Or a comer-by be seen
Swinging in a palanquin;
Where among the desert sands
Some deserted city stands,

All its children, sweep and prince,
Grown to manhood ages since,
Not a foot in street or house,
Not a stir of child or mouse,
And when kindly falls the night,
In all the town no spark of light.
There I'll come when I'm a man
With a camel caravan;
Light a fire in the gloom
Of some dusty dining-room;
See the pictures on the walls,
Heroes, fights and festivals;
And in a corner find the toys
Of the old Egyptian boys.

SINGING

Of speckled eggs the birdie sings
    And nests among the trees;
The sailor sings of ropes and things
    In ships upon the seas.

The children sing in far Japan,
    The children sing in Spain;
The organ with the organ man
    Is singing in the rain.

LOOKING FORWARD

When I am grown to man's estate
I shall be very proud and great,
And tell the other girls and boys
Not to meddle with my toys.

A GOOD PLAY

We built a ship upon the stairs
All made of the back-bedroom chairs,
And filled it full of sofa pillows
To go a-sailing on the billows.

We took a saw and several nails,
And water in the nursery pails;
And Tom said, 'Let us also take
An apple and a slice of cake';
Which was enough for Tom and me
To go a-sailing on, till tea.

We sailed along for days and days,
And had the very best of plays;
But Tom fell out and hurt his knee,
So there was no one left but me.

WHERE GO THE BOATS?

Dark brown is the river,
  Golden is the sand.
It flows along for ever,
  With trees on either hand.

Green leaves a-floating,
  Castles of the foam,
Boats of mine a-boating –
  Where will all come home?

On goes the river
  And out past the mill,
Away down the valley,
  Away down the hill.

Away down the river,
  A hundred miles or more,
Other little children
  Shall bring my boats ashore.

AUNTIE'S SKIRTS

Whenever Auntie moves around,
Her dresses make a curious sound;
They trail behind her up the floor,
And trundle after through the door.

THE LAND OF COUNTERPANE

When I was sick and lay a-bed,
I had two pillows at my head,
And all my toys beside me lay
To keep me happy all the day.

And sometimes for an hour or so
I watched my leaden soldiers go,
With different uniforms and drills,
Among the bed-clothes, through the hills;

And sometimes sent my ships in fleets
All up and down among the sheets;
Or brought my trees and houses out,
And planted cities all about.

I was the giant great and still
That sits upon the pillow-hill,
And sees before him, dale and plain,
The pleasant land of counterpane.

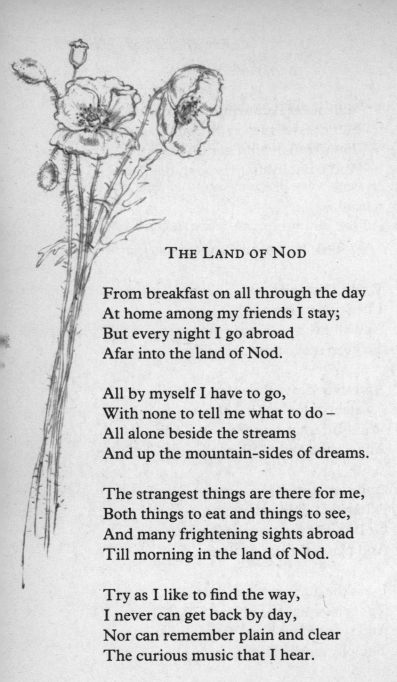

THE LAND OF NOD

From breakfast on all through the day
At home among my friends I stay;
But every night I go abroad
Afar into the land of Nod.

All by myself I have to go,
With none to tell me what to do –
All alone beside the streams
And up the mountain-sides of dreams.

The strangest things are there for me,
Both things to eat and things to see,
And many frightening sights abroad
Till morning in the land of Nod.

Try as I like to find the way,
I never can get back by day,
Nor can remember plain and clear
The curious music that I hear.

My Shadow

I have a little shadow that goes in and out with
    me,
And what can be the use of him is more than I
    can see.
He is very, very like me from the heels up to the
    head;
And I see him jump before me, when I jump into
    my bed.

The funniest thing about him is the way he likes
    to grow –
Not at all like proper children, which is always
    very slow;

For he sometimes shoots up taller like an india-
    rubber ball,
And he sometimes gets so little that there's none
    of him at all.

He hasn't got a notion of how children ought to
    play,
And can only make a fool of me in every sort of
    way.
He stays so close beside me, he's a coward you
    can see;
I'd think shame to stick to nursie as that shadow
    sticks to me!

One morning, very early, before the sun was up,
I rose and found the shining dew on every
    buttercup;
But my lazy little shadow, like an arrant sleepy-
    head,
Had stayed at home behind me and was fast asleep
    in bed.

SYSTEM

Every night my prayers I say,
And get my dinner every day;
And every day that I've been good,
I get an orange after food.

The child that is not clean and neat,
With lots of toys and things to eat,
He is a naughty child, I'm sure –
Or else his dear papa is poor.

A Good Boy

I woke before the morning, I was happy all the day,
I never said an ugly word, but smiled and stuck to play.

And now at last the sun is going down behind the wood,
And I am very happy, for I know that I've been good.

My bed is waiting cool and fresh, with linen smooth
    and fair,
And I must off to sleepsin-by, and not forget my
    prayer.

I know that, till to-morrow I shall see the sun arise,
No ugly dream shall fright my mind, no ugly sight
    my eyes,

But slumber hold me tightly till I waken in the dawn,
And hear the thrushes singing in the lilacs round
    the lawn.

ESCAPE AT BEDTIME

The lights from the parlour and kitchen shone
    out
    Through the blinds and the windows and bars;
And high overhead and all moving about,
    There were thousands of millions of stars.
There ne'er were such thousands of leaves on a
    tree,
    Nor of people in church or the Park,
As the crowds of the stars that looked down upon
    me,
    And that glittered and winked in the dark.

The Dog, and the Plough, and the Hunter, and
    all,
    And the star of the sailor, and Mars,
These shone in the sky, and the pail by the wall
    Would be half full of water and stars.
They saw me at last, and they chased me with
    cries,
    And they soon had me packed into bed;
But the glory kept shining and bright in my eyes,
    And the stars going round in my head.

MARCHING SONG

Bring the comb and play upon it!
   Marching, here we come!
Willie cocks his highland bonnet,
   Johnnie beats the drum.

Mary Jane commands the party,
   Peter leads the rear;
Feet in time, alert and hearty,
   Each a Grenadier!

All in the most martial manner
   Marching double-quick;
While the napkin like a banner
   Waves upon the stick!

THE COW

The friendly cow, all red and white,
  I love with all my heart:
She gives me cream with all her might,
  To eat with apple-tart.

She wanders lowing here and there,
  And yet she cannot stray,
All in the pleasant open air,
  The pleasant light of day;

And blown by all the winds that pass
  And wet with all the showers,
She walks among the meadow grass
  And eats the meadow flowers.

HAPPY THOUGHT

The world is so full
  of a number of things,
I'm sure we should all
  be as happy as kings.

The Wind

I saw you toss the kites on high
And blow the birds about the sky;
And all around I heard you pass,
Like ladies' skirts across the grass –
    O wind, a-blowing all day long,
    O wind, that sings so loud a song!

I saw the different things you did,
But always you yourself you hid.
I felt you push, I heard you call,
I could not see yourself at all –
    O wind, a-blowing all day long,
    O wind, that sings so loud a song!

O you that are so strong and cold,
O blower, are you young or old?
Are you a beast of field and tree,
Or just a stronger child than me?
    O wind, a-blowing all day long,
    O wind, that sings so loud a song!

KEEPSAKE MILL

Over the borders, a sin without pardon,
  Breaking the branches and crawling below,
Out through the breach in the wall of the garden,
  Down by the banks of the river, we go.

Here is the mill with the humming of thunder,
  Here is the weir with the wonder of foam,
Here is the sluice with the race running under –
  Marvellous places, though handy to home!

Sounds of the village grow stiller and stiller,
   Stiller the note of the birds on the hill;
Dusty and dim are the eyes of the miller,
   Deaf are his ears with the moil of the mill.

Years may go by, and the wheel in the river
   Wheel as it wheels for us, children, to-day,
Wheel and keep roaring and foaming for ever
   Long after all of the boys are away.

Home from the Indies, and home from the ocean,
   Heroes and soldiers we all shall come home;
Still we shall find the old mill-wheel in motion,
   Turning and churning that river to foam.

You with the bean that I gave when we
    quarrelled,
   I with your marble of Saturday last,
Honoured and old and all gaily apparelled,
   Here we shall meet and remember the past.

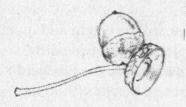

Good and Bad Children

Children, you are very little,
And your bones are very brittle;
If you would grow great and stately,
You must try to walk sedately.

You must still be bright and quiet,
And content with simple diet;
And remain, through all bewild'ring,
Innocent and honest children.

Happy hearts and happy faces,
Happy play in grassy places –
That was how, in ancient ages,
Children grew to kings and sages.

But the unkind and the unruly,
And the sort to eat unduly,
They must never hope for glory –
Theirs is quite a different story!

Cruel children, crying babies,
All grow up as geese and gabies,
Hated, as their age increases,
By their nephews and their nieces.

FOREIGN CHILDREN

Little Indian, Sioux or Crow,
Little frosty Eskimo,
Little Turk or Japanee,
O! don't you wish that you were me?

You have seen the scarlet trees
And the lions over seas;
You have eaten ostrich eggs,
And turned the turtles off their legs.

Such a life is very fine,
But it's not so nice as mine;
You must often, as you trod,
Have wearied *not* to be abroad.

You have curious things to eat,
I am fed on proper meat;
You must dwell beyond the foam,
But I am safe and live at home.

Little Indian, Sioux or Crow,
Little frosty Eskimo,
Little Turk or Japanee,
O! don't you wish that you were me?

THE SUN'S TRAVELS

The sun is not a-bed when I
At night upon my pillow lie;
Still round the earth his way he takes,
And morning after morning makes.

While here at home, in shining day,
We round the sunny garden play,
Each little Indian sleepy-head
Is being kissed and put to bed.

And when at eve I rise from tea,
Day dawns beyond the Atlantic Sea,
And all the children in the West
Are getting up and being dressed.

THE LAMPLIGHTER

My tea is nearly ready
   and the sun has left the sky;
It's time to take the window
   to see Leerie going by;
For every night at tea-time
   and before you take your seat,
With lantern and with ladder
   he comes posting up the street.

Now Tom would be a driver
   and Maria go to sea,
And my papa's a banker
   and as rich as he can be;
But I, when I am stronger
   and can choose what I'm to do,
O Leerie, I'll go round at night
   and light the lamps with you!

For we are very lucky,
   with a lamp before the door,
And Leerie stops to light it
   as he lights so many more;
And O! before you hurry by
   with ladder and with light,
O Leerie, see a little child
   and nod to him to-night!

My Bed is a Boat

My bed is like a little boat;
    Nurse helps me when I embark;
She girds me in my sailor's coat
    And starts me in the dark.

At night, I go on board and say
    Good-night to all my friends on shore;
I shut my eyes and sail away
    And see and hear no more.

And sometimes things to bed I take,
    As prudent sailors have to do;
Perhaps a slice of wedding-cake,
    Perhaps a toy or two.

All night across the dark we steer:
    But when the day returns at last,
Safe in my room, beside the pier,
    I find my vessel fast.

THE MOON

The moon has a face like the clock in the hall;
She shines on thieves on the garden wall,
On streets and fields and harbour quays,
And birdies asleep in the forks of the trees.

The squalling cat and the squeaking mouse,
The howling dog by the door of the house,
The bat that lies in bed at noon,
All love to be out by the light of the moon.

But all of the things that belong to the day
Cuddle to sleep to be out of her way;
And flowers and children close their eyes
Till up in the morning the sun shall rise.

THE SWING

How do you like to go up in a swing,
    Up in the air so blue?
Oh, I do think it the pleasantest thing
    Ever a child can do!

Up in the air and over the wall,
    Till I can see so wide,
Rivers and trees and cattle and all
    Over the countryside –

Till I look down on the garden green,
    Down on the roof so brown –
Up in the air I go flying again,
    Up in the air and down!

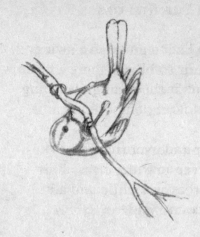

TIME TO RISE

A birdie with a yellow bill
Hopped upon the window sill.
Cocked his shining eye and said:
'Ain't you 'shamed, you sleepy-head?'

LOOKING-GLASS RIVER

Smooth it slides upon its travel,
  Here a wimple, there a gleam –
    O the clean gravel!
    O the smooth stream!

Sailing blossoms, silver fishes,
  Paven pools as clear as air –
    How a child wishes
    To live down there!

We can see our coloured faces
  Floating on the shaken pool
    Down in the cool places,
    Dim and very cool;

Till a wind or water wrinkle,
  Dipping marten, plumping trout,
    Spreads in a twinkle
    And blots all out.

See the rings pursue each other;
  All below grows black as night,
    Just as if mother
    Had blown out the light!

Patience, children, just a minute –
  See the spreading circles die;
    The stream and all in it
    Will clear by-and-by.

FAIRY BREAD

Come up here, O dusty feet!
   Here is fairy bread to eat.
Here in my retiring room,
   Children, you may dine
On the golden smell of broom
   And the shade of pine;
And when you have eaten well,
Fairy stories hear and tell.

FROM A RAILWAY CARRIAGE

Faster than fairies, faster than witches,
Bridges and houses, hedges and ditches;
And charging along like troops in a battle,
All through the meadows the horses and cattle:
All of the sights of the hill and the plain
Fly as thick as driving rain;
And ever again, in the wink of an eye,
Painted stations whistle by.

Here is a child who clambers and scrambles,
All by himself and gathering brambles;
Here is a tramp who stands and gazes;
And there is the green for stringing the daisies!
Here is a cart run away in the road
Lumping along with man and load;
And here is a mill, and there is a river:
Each a glimpse and gone for ever!

WINTER-TIME

Late lies the wintry sun a-bed,
A frosty, fiery sleepy-head;
Blinks but an hour or two; and then,
A blood-red orange, sets again.

Before the stars have left the skies,
At morning in the dark I rise;
And shivering in my nakedness,
By the cold candle, bathe and dress.

Close by the jolly fire I sit
To warm my frozen bones a bit;
Or with a reindeer-sled, explore
The colder countries round the door.

When, to go out, my nurse doth wrap
Me in my comforter and cap:
The cold wind burns my face, and blows
Its frosty pepper up my nose.

Black are my steps on silver sod;
Thick blows my frosty breath abroad;
And tree and house, and hill and lake,
Are frosted like a wedding-cake.

THE HAYLOFT

Through all the pleasant meadow-side
   The grass grew shoulder-high,
Till the shining scythes went far and wide
   And cut it down to dry.

These green and sweetly smelling drops
   They led in waggons home;
And they piled them here in mountain tops
   For mountaineers to roam.

Here is Mount Clear, Mount Rusty-Nail,
   Mount Eagle and Mount High; –
The mice that in these mountains dwell,
   No happier are than I!

O what a joy to clamber there,
   O what a place for play,
With the sweet, the dim, the dusty air,
   The happy hills of hay.

FAREWELL TO THE FARM

The coach is at the door at last;
The eager children, mounting fast
And kissing hands, in chorus sing:
Good-bye, good-bye, to everything!

To house and garden, field and lawn,
The meadow-gates we swang upon,
To pump and stable, tree and swing,
Good-bye, good-bye, to everything!

And fare you well for evermore,
O ladder at the hayloft door,
O hayloft where the cobwebs cling,
Good-bye, good-bye, to everything!

Crack goes the whip, and off we go;
The trees and houses smaller grow;
Last, round the woody turn we swing:
Good-bye, good-bye, to everything!

NORTH-WEST PASSAGE

1. *Good Night*

When the bright lamp is carried in,
The sunless hours again begin;
O'er all without, in field and lane,
The haunted night returns again.

Now we behold the embers flee
About the firelit hearth; and see
Our faces painted as we pass,
Like pictures, on the window-glass.

Must we to bed indeed? Well then,
Let us arise and go like men,
And face with an undaunted tread
The long black passage up to bed.

Farewell, O brother, sister, sire!
O pleasant party round the fire!
The songs you sing, the tales you tell,
Till far to-morrow, fare ye well!

2. *Shadow March*

All round the house is the jet-black night;
  It stares through the window-pane;
It crawls in the corners, hiding from the light,
  And it moves with the moving flame.

Now my little heart goes a-beating like a drum,
  With the breath of the Bogie in my hair;
And all round the candle the crooked shadows come
  And go marching along up the stair.

The shadow of the balusters, the shadow of the
    lamp,
  The shadow of the child that goes to bed –
All the wicked shadows coming, tramp, tramp,
    tramp,
  With the black light overhead.

3. *In Port*

  Last, to the chamber where I lie
  My fearful footsteps patter nigh,
  And come from out the cold and gloom
  Into my warm and cheerful room.

  There, safe arrived, we turn about
  To keep the coming shadows out,
  And close the happy door at last
  On all the perils that we past.

  Then, when mamma goes by to bed,
  She shall come in with tip-toed tread,
  And see me lying warm and fast
  And in the Land of Nod at last.

THE CHILD ALONE

THE UNSEEN PLAYMATE

When children are playing alone on the green,
In comes the playmate that never was seen.
When children are happy and lonely and good,
The Friend of the Children comes out of the
    wood.

Nobody heard him and nobody saw,
His is a picture you never could draw,
But he's sure to be present, abroad or at home,
When children are happy and playing alone.

He lies in the laurels, he runs on the grass,
He sings when you tinkle the musical glass;
Whene'er you are happy and cannot tell why,
The Friend of the Children is sure to be by!

He loves to be little, he hates to be big,
'Tis he that inhabits the caves that you dig;
'Tis he when you play with your soldiers of tin
That sides with the Frenchmen and never can
      win.

'Tis he, when at night you go off to your bed,
Bids you go to your sleep and not trouble your
      head;
For wherever they're lying, in cupboard or shelf,
'Tis he will take care of your playthings himself!

MY SHIP AND I

O it's I that am the captain of a tidy little ship,
   Of a ship that goes a-sailing on the pond;
And my ship it keeps a-turning all around and all
     about;
But when I'm a little older, I shall find the secret
     out
   How to send my vessel sailing on beyond.

For I mean to grow as little as the dolly at the
     helm,
   And the dolly I intend to come alive;
And with him beside to help me, it's a-sailing I
     shall go,
It's a sailing on the water, when the jolly breezes
     blow
   And the vessel goes a divie-divie dive.

O it's then you'll see me sailing through the rushes
    and the reeds,
  And you'll hear the water singing at the prow;
For beside the dolly sailor, I'm to voyage and
    explore,
To land upon the island where no dolly was
    before,
  And to fire the penny cannon in the bow.

My Kingdom

Down by a shining water well
I found a very little dell,
  No higher than my head.
The heather and the gorse about
In summer bloom were coming out,
  Some yellow and some red.

I called the little pool a sea;
The little hills were big to me;
  For I am very small.
I made a boat, I made a town,
I searched the caverns up and down,
  And named them one and all.

And all about was mine, I said,
The little sparrows overhead,
   The little minnows too.
This was the world and I was king;
For me the bees came by to sing,
   For me the swallows flew.

I played there were no deeper seas,
Nor any wider plains than these,
   No other kings than me.
At last I heard my mother call
Out from the house at even-fall,
   To call me home to tea.

And I must rise and leave my dell,
And leave my dimpled water well,
   And leave my heather blooms.
Alas! and as my home I neared,
How very big my nurse appeared,
   How great and cool the rooms!

PICTURE-BOOKS IN WINTER

Summer fading, winter comes –
Frosty mornings, tingling thumbs,
Window robins, winter rooks,
And the picture story-books.

Water now is turned to stone
Nurse and I can walk upon;
Still we find the flowing brooks
In the picture story-books.

All the pretty things put by,
Wait upon the children's eye,
Sheep and shepherds, trees and crooks,
In the picture story-books.

We may see how all things are,
Seas and cities, near and far,
And the flying fairies' looks,
In the picture story-books.

How am I to sing your praise,
Happy chimney-corner days,
Sitting safe in nursery nooks,
Reading picture story-books?

MY TREASURES

These nuts that I keep in the back of the nest
Where all my lead soldiers are lying at rest,
Were gathered in autumn by nursie and me
In a wood with a well by the side of the sea.

This whistle we made (and how clearly it
    sounds!)
By the side of a field at the end of the grounds.
Of a branch of a plane, with a knife of my own,
It was nursie who made it, and nursie alone!

The stone, with the white and the yellow and
    grey,
We discovered I cannot tell *how* far away;
And I carried it back although weary and cold,
For though father denies it, I'm sure it is gold.

But of all of my treasures the last is the king,
For there's very few children possess such a
    thing;
And that is a chisel, both handle and blade,
Which a man who was really a carpenter made.

BLOCK CITY

What are you able to build with your blocks?
Castle and palaces, temples and docks.
Rain may keep raining, and others go roam,
But I can be happy and building at home.

Let the sofa be mountains, the carpet be sea,
There I'll establish a city for me:
A kirk and a mill and a palace beside,
And a harbour as well where my vessels may ride.

Great is the palace with pillar and wall,
A sort of a tower on the top of it all,
And steps coming down in an orderly way
To where my toy vessels lie safe in the bay.

This one is sailing and that one is moored:
Hark to the song of the sailors on board!
And see on the steps of my palace, the kings
Coming and going with presents and things!

Now I have done with it, down let it go!
All in a moment the town is laid low.
Block upon block lying scattered and free,
What is there left of my town by the sea?

Yet as I saw it, I see it again,
The kirk and the palace, the ships and the men,
And as long as I live, and where'er I may be,
I'll always remember my town by the sea.

THE LAND OF STORY-BOOKS

At evening when the lamp is lit,
Around the fire my parents sit;
They sit at home and talk and sing,
And do not play at anything.

Now, with my little gun, I crawl
All in the dark along the wall,
And follow round the forest track
Away behind the sofa back.

There, in the night, where none can spy,
All in my hunter's camp I lie,
And play at books that I have read
Till it is time to go to bed.

These are the hills, these are the woods,
These are my starry solitudes;
And there the river by whose brink
The roaring lions come to drink.

I see the others far away
As if in firelit camp they lay,
And I, like to an Indian scout,
Around their party prowled about.

So, when my nurse comes in for me,
Home I return across the sea,
And go to bed with backward looks
At my dear land of Story-books.

ARMIES IN THE FIRE

The lamps now glitter down the street;
Faintly sound the falling feet;
And the blue even slowly falls
About the garden trees and walls.

Now in the falling of the gloom
The red fire paints the empty room:
And warmly on the roof it looks,
And flickers on the backs of books.

Armies march by tower and spire
Of cities blazing, in the fire;
Till as I gaze with staring eyes,
The armies fade, the lustre dies.

Then once again the glow returns;
Again the phantom city burns;
And down the red-hot valley, lo!
The phantom armies marching go!

Blinking embers, tell me true,
Where are those armies marching to,
And what the burning city is
That crumbles in your furnaces!

THE LITTLE LAND

When at home alone I sit
And am very tired of it,
I have just to shut my eyes
To go sailing through the skies –
To go sailing far away
To the pleasant Land of Play;
To the fairy land afar
Where the Little People are;
Where the clover-tops are trees,
And the rain-pools are the seas,
And the leaves like little ships
Sail about on tiny trips;
And above the daisy tree
 Through the grasses,
High o'erhead the Bumble Bee
 Hums and passes.

In that forest to and fro
I can wander, I can go;
See the spider and the fly,
And the ants go marching by
Carrying parcels with their feet
Down the green and grassy street.
I can in the sorrel sit,
Where the ladybird alit.
I can climb the jointed grass,
   And on high
See the greater swallows pass
   In the sky,
And the round sun rolling by
Heeding no such things as I.

Through that forest I can pass
Till, as in a looking glass,
Humming fly and daisy tree
And my tiny self I see,
Painted very clear and neat
On the rain-pool at my feet.
Should a leaflet come to land
Drifting near to where I stand,
Straight I'll board that tiny boat
Round the rain-pool sea to float.

Little thoughtful creatures sit
On the grassy coast of it.
Little things with lovely eyes
See me sailing with surprise.
Some are clad in armour green –
(These have sure to battle been!) –
Some are pied with every hue,
Black and crimson, gold and blue;
Some have wings and swift are gone;
But they all look kindly on.

When my eyes I once again
Open, and see all things plain:
High bare walls, great bare floor;
Great big knobs on drawer and door;
Great big people perched on chairs,
Stitching tucks and mending tears,
Each a hill that I could climb,
And talking nonsense all the time –
  O dear me,
  That I could be
A sailor on the rain-pool sea,
A climber in the clover tree,
And just come back, a sleepy-head,
Late at night to go to bed.

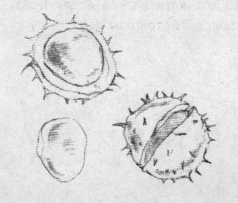

GARDEN DAYS

NIGHT AND DAY

When the golden day is done,
  Through the closing portal,
Child and garden, flower and sun,
  Vanish all things mortal.

As the blinding shadows fall,
  As the rays diminish,
Under evening's cloak, they all
  Roll away and vanish.

Garden darkened, daisy shut,
  Child in bed, they slumber –
Glow-worm in the highway rut,
  Mice among the lumber.

In the darkness houses shine,
　　Parents move with candles;
Till, on all, the night divine
　　Turns the bedroom handles.

Till at last the day begins
　　In the east a-breaking,
In the hedges and the whins
　　Sleeping birds a-waking.

In the darkness shapes of things,
　　Houses, trees, and hedges,
Clearer grow; and sparrow's wings
　　Beat on window ledges.

These shall wake the yawning maid;
　　She the door shall open –
Finding dew on garden glade
　　And the morning broken.

There my garden grows again
　　Green and rosy painted,
As at eve behind the pane
　　From my eyes it fainted.

Just as it was shut away,
   Toy-like, in the even,
Here I see it glow with day
   Under glowing heaven.

Every path and every plot,
   Every bush of roses,
Every blue forget-me-not
   Where the dew reposes,

'Up!' they cry, 'the day is come
   On the smiling valleys;
We have beat the morning drum;
   Playmate, join your allies!'

NEST EGGS

Birds all the sunny day
   Flutter and quarrel
Here in the arbour-like
   Tent of the laurel.

Here in the fork
   The brown nest is seated;
Four little blue eggs
   The mother keeps heated.

While we stand watching her,
   Staring like gabies,
Safe in each egg are the
   Bird's little babies.

Soon the frail eggs they shall
   Chip, and upspringing
Make all the April woods
   Merry with singing.

Younger than we are,
   O children, and frailer,
Soon in blue air they'll be
   Singer and sailor.

We, so much older,
   Taller and stronger,
We shall look down on the
   Birdies no longer.

They shall go flying
    With musical speeches
High overhead in the
    Tops of the beeches.

In spite of our wisdom
    And sensible talking,
We on our feet must go
    Plodding and walking.

THE FLOWERS

All the names I know from nurse:
Gardener's garters, Shepherd's purse,
Bachelor's buttons, Lady's smock,
And the Lady Hollyhock.

Fairy places, fairy things,
Fairy woods where the wild bee wings,
Tiny trees for tiny dames –
These must all be fairy names!

Tiny woods below whose boughs
Shady fairies weave a house;
Tiny tree-tops, rose or thyme,
Where the braver fairies climb!

Fair are grown-up people's trees,
But the fairest woods are these;
Where if I were not so tall,
I should live for good and all.

SUMMER SUN

Great is the sun, and wide he goes
Through empty heaven without repose;
And in the blue and glowing days
More thick than rain he showers his rays.

Though closer still the blinds we pull
To keep the shady parlour cool,
Yet he will find a chink or two
To slip his golden fingers through.

The dusty attic, spider-clad,
He, through the keyhole, maketh glad;
And through the broken edge of tiles,
Into the laddered hayloft smiles.

Meantime his golden face around
He bares to all the garden ground,
And sheds a warm and glittering look
Among the ivy's inmost nook.

Above the hills, along the blue
Round the bright air with footing true.
To please the child, to paint the rose,
The gardener of the World, he goes.

THE DUMB SOLDIER

When the grass was closely mown,
Walking on the lawn alone,
In the turf a hole I found
And hid a soldier underground.

Spring and daisies came apace;
Grasses hide my hiding-place;
Grasses run like a green sea
O'er the lawn up to my knee.

Under grass alone he lies,
Looking up with leaden eyes,
Scarlet coat and pointed gun,
To the stars and to the sun.

When the grass is ripe like grain,
When the scythe is stoned again,
When the lawn is shaven clear,
Then my hole shall reappear.

I shall find him, never fear,
I shall find my grenadier;
But for all that's gone and come,
I shall find my soldier dumb.

He has lived, a little thing,
In the grassy woods of spring;
Done, if he could tell me true,
Just as I should like to do.

He has seen the starry hours
And the springing of the flowers;
And the fairy things that pass
In the forests of the grass.

In the silence he has heard
Talking bee and ladybird,
And the butterfly has flown
O'er him as he lay alone.

Not a word will he disclose,
Not a word of all he knows.
I must lay him on the shelf,
And make up the tale myself.

Autumn Fires

In the other gardens
   And all up the vale,
From the autumn bonfires
   See the smoke trail!

Pleasant summer over
   And all the summer flowers,
The red fire blazes,
   The grey smoke towers.

Sing a song of seasons!
   Something bright in all!
Flowers in the summer,
   Fires in the fall!

THE GARDENER

The gardener does not love to talk,
He makes me keep the gravel walk;
And when he puts his tools away;
He locks the door and takes the key.

Away behind the currant row
Where no one else but cook may go,
Far in the plots, I see him dig,
Old and serious, brown and big.

He digs the flowers, green, red, and blue,
Nor wishes to be spoken to.
He digs the flowers and cuts the hay,
And never seems to want to play.

Silly gardener! summer goes,
And winter comes with pinching toes,
When in the garden bare and brown
You must lay your barrow down.

Well now, and while the summer stays,
To profit by these garden days,
O how much wiser you would be
To play at Indian wars with me!

HISTORICAL ASSOCIATIONS

Dear Uncle Jim, this garden ground
That now you smoke your pipe around
Has seen immortal actions done
And valiant battles lost and won.

Here we had best on tip-toe tread,
While I for safety march ahead,
For this is that enchanted ground
Where all who loiter slumber sound.

Here is the sea, here is the sand,
Here is simple Shepherd's Land,
Here are the fairy hollyhocks,
And there are Ali Baba's rocks.

But yonder, see! apart and high,
Frozen Siberia lies; where I,
With Robert Bruce and William Tell,
Was bound by an enchanter's spell.

There, then, awhile in chains we lay,
In wintry dungeons, far from day;
But ris'n at length, with might and main,
Our iron fetters burst in twain,

Then all the horns were blown in town;
And, to the ramparts clanging down,
All the giants leaped to horse
And charged behind us through the gorse.

On we rode, the others and I,
Over the mountains blue, and by
The Silent River, the sounding sea,
And the robber woods of Tartary.

A thousand miles we galloped fast,
And down the witches' lane we passed,
And rode amain, with brandished sword,
Up to the middle, through the ford.

Last we drew rein – a weary three –
Upon the lawn, in time for tea,
And from our steeds alighted down
Before the gates of Babylon.

ENVOYS

To Willie and Henrietta

If two may read aright
These rhymes of old delight
And house and garden play,
You two, my cousins, and you only, may.

You in a garden green
With me were king and queen,
Were hunter, soldier, tar,
And all the thousand things that children are.

Now in the elders' seat
We rest with quiet feet,
And from the window-bay
We watch the children, our successors, play.

'Time was,' the golden head
Irrevocably said;
But time which none can bind,
While flowing fast away, leaves love behind.

TO MY MOTHER

You too, my mother, read my rhymes
For the love of unforgotten times,
And you may chance to hear once more
The little feet along the floor.

To Auntie

Chief of our aunts – not only I,
But all your dozen of nurslings cry –
What did the other children do?
And what were childhood, wanting you?

To Minnie

The red room with the giant bed
Where none but elders laid their head;
The little room where you and I
Did for awhile together lie
And, simple suitor, I your hand
In decent marriage did demand;
The great day nursery, best of all,
With pictures pasted on the wall
And leaves upon the blind –
A pleasant room wherein to wake
And hear the leafy garden shake
And rustle in the wind –
And pleasant there to lie in bed
And see the pictures overhead –
The wars about Sebastopol,
The grinning guns along the wall,
The daring escalade,
The plunging ships, the bleating sheep,
The happy children ankle-deep
And laughing as they wade;
All these are vanished clean away,
And the old manse is changed to-day;
It wears an altered face
And shields a stranger race.

The river, on from mill to mill,
Flows past our childhood's garden still;
But ah! we children never more
Shall watch it from the water-door!
Below the yew – it still is there –
Our phantom voices haunt the air
As we were still at play,
And I can hear them call and say:
'*How far is it to Babylon?*'

Ah, far enough, my dear,
Far, far enough from here –
Yet you have farther gone!
'*Can I get there by candlelight?*'
So goes the old refrain.
I do not know – perchance you might –
But only, children, hear it right,
Ah, never to return again!
The eternal dawn, beyond a doubt,
Shall break on hill and plain,
And put all stars and candles out,
Ere we be young again.

To you in distant India, these
I send across the seas,
Nor count it far across.
For which of us forgets
The Indian cabinets,
The bones of antelope, the wings of albatross.
The pied and painted birds and beans,
The junks and bangles, beads and screens,
The gods and sacred bells,
And the loud-humming, twisted shells?
The level of the parlour floor
Was honest, homely, Scottish shore;
But when we climbed upon a chair,
Behold the gorgeous East was there!

Be this a fable; and behold
Me in the parlour as of old,
And Minnie just above me set
In the quaint Indian cabinet!
Smiling and kind, you grace a shelf
Too high for me to reach myself.
Reach down a hand, my dear, and take
These rhymes for old acquaintance' sake.

To My Name-child

1

Some day soon this rhyming volume, if you learn
    with proper speed,
Little Louis Sanchez, will be given you to read.
Then shall you discover, that your name was
    printed down
By the English printers, long before, in London
    town.

In the great and busy city where the East and
    West are met,
All the little letters did the English printer set;
While you thought of nothing, and were still too
    young to play,
Foreign people thought of you in places far away.

Ay, and while you slept, a baby, over all the
    English lands
Other little children took the volume in their
    hands;
Other children questioned, in their homes across
    the seas:
Who was Little Louis, won't you tell us, mother,
    please?

2

Now that you have spelt your lesson, lay it down
    and go and play,
Seeking shells and seaweed on the sands of
    Monterey,
Watching all the mighty whalebones, lying buried
    by the breeze,
Tiny sandy-pipers, and the huge Pacific seas.

And remember in your playing, as the sea-fog
    rolls to you,
Long ere you could read it, how I told you what
    to do;
And that while you thought of no one, nearly half
    the world away
Some one thought of Louis on the beach of
    Monterey!

To Any Reader

As from the house your mother sees
You playing round the garden trees,
So you may see, if you will look
Through the windows of this book,
Another child, far, far away,
And in another garden, play.
But do not think you can at all,
By knocking on the window, call
That child to hear you. He intent
Is all on his play-business bent.
He does not hear; he will not look,
Nor yet be lured out of his book.
For, long ago, the truth to say,
He has grown up and gone away,
And it is but a child of air
That lingers in the garden there.

INDEX OF FIRST LINES

A birdie with a yellow bill, 40
A child should always say what's true, 5
All night long, and every night, 4
All round the house is the jet-black night, 50
All the names I know from nurse, 83
As from the house your mother sees, 104
At evening when the lamp is lit, 67

Birds all the sunny day, 80
Bring the comb and play upon it, 24

Chief of our aunts – not only I, 97
Children, you are very little, 30
Come up here, O dusty feet, 43

Dark brown is the river, 16
Dear Uncle Jim, this garden ground, 89
Down by a shining water well, 60

Every night my prayers I say, 21

Faster than fairies, faster than witches, 44
From breakfast on all through the day, 18

Great is the sun, and wide he goes, 84

How do you like to go up in a swing, 39

I have a little shadow that goes in and out with me, 19
I saw you toss the kites on high, 27
I should like to rise and go, 11
I woke before the morning, I was happy all the day, 22

If two may read aright, 95
In the other gardens, 87
In winter I get up at night, 1
It is very nice to think, 2

Last, to the chamber where I lie, 52
Late lies the wintry sun a-bed, 45
Little Indian, Sioux or Crow, 33

My bed is like a little boat, 37
My tea is nearly ready and the sun has left the sky, 35

O it's I that am the captain of a tidy little ship, 59
Of speckled eggs the birdie sings, 14
Over the borders, a sin without pardon, 28

Smooth it slides upon its travel, 41
Some day soon this rhyming volume, if you learn with
   proper speed, 102
Summer fading, winter comes, 62

The coach is at the door at last, 48
The friendly cow, all red and white, 25
The gardener does not love to talk, 88
The lamps now glitter down the street, 69
The lights from the parlour and kitchen shone out, 23
The moon has a face like the clock in the hall, 38
The red room with the giant bed, 98
The rain is raining all around, 64
The sun is not a-bed when I, 34
The world is so full of a number of things, 26
These nuts, that I keep in the back of the nest, 64
Three of us afloat in the meadow by the swing, 7
Through all the pleasant meadow-side, 47

Up into the cherry-tree, 8

We built a ship upon the stairs, 15
What are you able to build with your blocks? 65
When at home alone I sit, 70
When children are playing alone on the green, 57
When I am grown to man's estate, 15
When I was down beside the sea, 3
When I was sick and lay a-bed, 17
When the bright lamp is carried in, 50
When the golden day is done, 77
When the grass was closely mown, 85
Whenever Auntie moves around, 17
Whenever the moon and stars are set, 10

You too, my mother, read my rhymes, 96

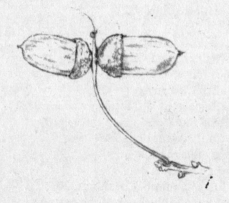

*Also by Robert Louis Stevenson
in Puffin Classics*

KIDNAPPED

Young David Balfour came to the sinister House of Shaws to claim his inheritance. Instead, he found himself kidnapped, the victim of a plot to murder him. With the help of daring rebel Alan Breck, David escapes, only to get mixed up in a desperate adventure – suspected of murder himself, and hunted across the Scottish moors.

TREASURE ISLAND

When Jim Hawkins picks up the oilskin packet from Captain Flint's sea chest, he has no idea that here lies the key to untold wealth – a treasure map. He sails on the *Hispaniola* as cabin-boy, with the awesome Long John Silver as ship's cook and the rest of the shifty crew, and embarks on an extraordinary and dangerous quest to find the buried treasure.

Dr Jekyll is a respectable, well-liked scientist —
until a secret experiment goes hideously wrong,
and he is plunged into a nightmare existence as
the monstrous Mr Hyde . . . And the hero of *The
Suicide Club* gets just as entangled with a sinister
secret society when he unwisely indulges his taste
for adventure.